My Name is Henley
(My life and times as a rescued dog)

By Henley Harrison West

Typed by Judith Kristen

"Hey Jude"
John Lennon and Paul McCartney
Copyright 1968 (Renewed) Sony/ATV Tunes LLC. All rights administered by Sony/ATV Music Publishing, 8 Music Square West, Nashville, TN 37203. All rights reserved. Used by permission.

"Memory"
Lyrics from the musical, "CATS" credited to: Eliot/Rice/Webber
"CATS" from T.S. Eliot Old Possum's Book of Practical Cats - 1939
All rights reserved. Used by permission.
Faber and Faber, Ltd. 3 Queen Square, London. WC1N 3AU

"Disney" is a registered trademark of The Walt Disney Company.

ISBN: 978-0-9800448-0-5

Printed in the United States of America
This book is printed on acid-free paper.

Cover Design: Dr. Louis Castelli and David Adams
Aquinas & Krone logo designed by: Tim Litostansky
Editor: Alex Hill
Photos: Jude West
Photo edits: Jonathan Reed West
This book is partially fictionalized.
First published by Aquinas & Krone Publishing, LLC 8/16/2007
Second Printing: November 16th, 2007

Please visit: www.judithkristen.com

Henley apologizes to Dr. Lou for the absence of Grammar Cat and Syntax Dog.

For Cristina!! ☺

This book is dedicated to
Everyone who loves animals
as much as I do.

Henley

Judith Kristen

My Name is Henley
(My life and times as a rescued dog)

By Henley Harrison West
Typed by Judith Kristen

Prologue

As the title of the book says: *My name is Henley*.

Not only is my name Henley, but I'm an Old English Sheepdog.

A Shaggy Dog… The Shaggy D.A. … A Disney Dog… I hear all those names.

Actually the thing I hear most is, "Can he see?"

For the record, I see rather well.

As for my 'Old' status in the *Old* English Sheepdog title, I'm 'gettin' up there' according to my vet, Dr. Vaughn.

Now I realize I'll be ten years old next March, and most of my fellow sheepherders bite the dust around that time… but not me. *I* have plans!

I guess maybe it's because my life started out in such a scary way that when things finally turned around for me, I embraced everything that came along… even cats!

Chapter One

I was born on March 10th, 1998, in Lancaster, Pennsylvania, in a place I heard them call a puppy mill. The people who ran the place weren't very nice, but my parents were wonderful. Dad was a proud herder who used to talk about being related to many a famous AKC champion. He was magnificent looking.

Mom wasn't from such strong lineage, but she sure was beautiful, and better yet, she was very kind and loving to all of her pups.

I was taken from my parents when I was barely six weeks old, and although there were eleven other siblings that went along with me, I really felt the loss of my mom and dad. I had nine very rough and tumble brothers and two very aggressive sisters, so I was kind of the odd dog out, if you know what I mean – sensitive… needy… the baby… something the puppy mill people called, 'the runt.'

On April 22nd of that year, we were all sent to a place that looked like a nice farm house from the front of the dwelling, but we didn't get to live there. We got stuck in the back yard in what I can only describe as a mud pen.

The water was never clean, the food was hard and tasted terrible, my baby teeth hurt, my hair was a mess, and my skin was always really itchy.

I'd cry for help when I'd see Cedra, the farm owner's wife, but all she ever did was tell me to, "Hush," and, "Be quiet, or Ralph will come out here and give you a whippin'!"

I wasn't sure what a whippin' was, but by the tone of her voice it didn't sound like something I'd particularly care for.

Now that I think about it, my brothers and sisters were starting to look a bit scruffy, too. But every now and then, Cedra or Ralph would come and take three or four of my siblings and disappear back into the nice house. A few hours later, they would come back to the pen, their hair all nice and clean... but one member of my family was always missing.

My youngest sister said to me, *"Cedra gave us a bath and fed us some good food."*

"She did?"

"Yup. And... and then Ralph invited people to... to come by and visit with us."

"Visit?"

"Yeah! And those people were great! They played ball with us, and held us, and..."

"Wow! Then what?"

"Well, then... then, one of those people said, 'We'll take him.'"

"'Take him?'"

"Yup. And then the new people left, they took our brother along with them, and the rest of us came back here to the pen."

"And that's it?"

"Yup. That's it."

Day by day this would happen until finally there was only me and two of my brothers left.

Both of them had already been to the house, they had played ball, seen the new people, and had some really good food *and* a nice, warm, sudsy bath.

I never did.

I was still too scraggly, still too itchy, and, as Ralph would always say when he looked at me, "Too ugly. Ya never make a dime off the runt!"

One chilly spring morning, my two brothers were taken into the nice house and we said our goodbyes to each other. I really expected to see at least one of them, if not both of them, come back to the pen so we could play together and be as much of a family as possible, considering how our numbers had dwindled... but neither one came back.

Not one.

I was alone in that mud pen for over two weeks.

The water got dirtier.

The food had bugs crawling around in it.

And my once beautiful shaggy sheepdog fur was all but rubbed right off my body. I was itchy from my head to my toes.

And I was so lonely I felt as if my heart would break.

Sixteen days into my exile came a horrible thunderstorm. I was in the mud pen and it was getting muddier by the minute. I was afraid I would drown. Ralph had tied me to the old wooden fence with a fraying rope collar and a rusty chain. The collar was tight around my neck and it was hard for me to swallow sometimes. I could barely move two feet in any direction.

I cried and howled and howled and cried.

I heard Cedra yelling at Ralph to bring me in, but he wouldn't allow it.

"IT'S JUST A DUMB ANIMAL!!!!" he yelled back at her.

I cringed at the sound of his voice.

I cried all night long.

I was *so* scared.

The thunderstorm passed away in the middle of the night, but I could still hear it in my head.

The day after the storm, Cedra and Ralph went for a ride in their truck. I was hoping they would come back with some good food for me, change the rain water in my bowl, and bring me some medicine for my itchy skin... but I never saw them again.

I had been abandoned and left to die.

I tried not to cry at night, but it was hard not to. I drank dirty water, slept a lot, ate a few bugs out of the mud, and thought about the nice days I had had with my mother and father... those days when my family was together... a loving, happy, and healthy pack.

Two days later I woke up to the sound of a kind voice.

"You poor little thing."

I looked up and saw a woman with a kind face and big blue eyes staring down at me.

I sat up as straight as I could and did my best to look like the dignified sheepdog that I was, but that was kinda hard to do with red and pink blotchy skin, no hair, and mud caked all over my feet.

She started to pick me up.

I talked to her inside my head. *Noooooooo!!!! You'll get all dirty and then you'll get mad and won't take me out of here! Put me down!!!!*

I squirmed and wiggled but somehow she didn't care about the mud all over her pretty eyelet dress.

"There, there, little boy... you're going to be all right now."

She looked at me with those soft blue eyes, and somewhere deep within my soul, I really believed that I would be.

Chapter Two

The woman whose dress I had muddied was named Myra Glick. Myra helped run an animal rescue shelter in northern New Jersey. She was compassionate... sweet... kind. You couldn't ask for a better friend.

Myra and I left Ralph and Cedra's farm and headed right to her friend's office. His name was Joel and, lucky for me, he was a veterinarian! Dr. Joel gave me a bath, some nice-tasting food, clean water, shots, vitamins, and some cream and medicine for my itchy skin. I felt wonderful!

"He'll be fine, Myra."

"Do you really think so?"

"Well, he's a runt, you can't expect miracles, but..."

"I know," she smiled. "Just find him a nice family to live with and the battle is half won."

He nodded and smiled at her. "That's the ticket!"

Myra scooped my clean, un-itchy self, up into her arms, took me out to her car, and then placed me on a soft blue and white blanket.

I slept all the way from Lancaster to Hoboken.

Chapter Three

This is a mighty fine place, I thought as Myra gave me the royal tour.

She held me in her arms as we walked around the shelter.

The other dogs were in cages, but the metal was really clean and very shiny. The water and food looked nice and fresh, everyone was happy, and they all wagged their tails as Myra and I walked by.

"Hi, there, young fella!" a large bloodhound voiced to me.

Then a dog that looked like a mix of 800 things barked, *"You'll like it here. They treat you well and I hear we're all gonna get nice families to take good care of us!"*

I looked up at Myra with love in my eyes and gave her a big kiss right on the face.

She smiled at me. "Come on, Boy, I think I have just the right mom for you."

Myra held me in her arms all the way into her office and then gently placed me on the floor. She picked up a contraption later identified to me as a telephone and she called someone. I only got to hear one side of the dialogue, but I liked what I heard.

"Hi, Jude! … It's a puppy. … A male. … Well, yes, he does have some health issues, but they should all be cleared up with the medication he has. … He's adorable. … A little needy, but … Oh, Judy, that's wonderful! … Tuesday? Great! We'll see you then!"

Now as you may or may not know: sheepdogs don't have tails. We're either born without them, or get them 'docked' at the vet when we're tiny puppies. I was born without a tail. Most people can easily tell when a dog is happy because the dog wags its tail. Sheepdogs can only wag their butts.

Well, when I heard that conversation, I wagged my butt so hard that I knocked myself over.

Myra laughed and picked me up off the floor.

"You're going to have a wonderful home, Boy! And you only have to wait until Tuesday!"

I looked at her and turned my head from right to left. *Tuesday? When is Tuesday? WHAT is Tuesday?!*

People underestimate themselves when it comes to instincts. Myra picked up on my feelings right away and smiled, "It's only three days away, little fella… just three more days!"

Chapter Four

I guess it was because I was still such a needy puppy that I got just a little extra special treatment at the shelter. In the daytime, I got to walk around Myra's office, and at night, I didn't have to go into a cage like the other dogs. I got to go home with Miss Myra!

Just as we were leaving that night, Stella, another one of the people who worked at the shelter, was walking my friend, the '800 kinds of dog' dog.

"I got a family, Boy!"

"Did you?!"

"I sure did! I'm goin' home right now! Stella's driving me there!"

"You met them already?"

"Yup. And they loved me! They came by today and we played together and they gave me treats. Look! I even got a collar with my name on it!"

"Wow! What's your name?!"

"Sparky."

Stella opened the car door. "Hop in, Sweetheart! You're goin' home!"

Sparky wagged his tail at me.

I wagged my butt.

"So long, young fella! Good luck to you!"
"So long, Sparky! Good luck to you, too!"

Chapter Five

As Myra and I drove to her house, I lay there on my nice blue and white blanket, thinking about what Sparky had said to me, you know, about his new family. *"They loved me!"* he said.

I took a look at my reflection in the shiny glove box – no hair, sad eyes, mottled skin...

I sighed. ...*Who could love this?!*

Once again, Myra picked up on my feelings, smiled down at me and said, "Your new mom is going to be crazy about you. You're a sweet dog and she needs some company. She'll love you to pieces."

I lifted up my head in interest.

"And, Fella... she knows *all* about sheepdogs! She's had sheepdogs all of her life."

She has?

"The last one died eight years ago."

That's a long time.

"She couldn't get another one because she was raising a grandchild who had lots of allergies."

People are allergic to dogs?!

"The little girl just moved back with her father and..."

Can dogs get allergic to people?!!

"Well, I guess you could say that the timing is right for both of you."

What did you say her name was?

Again, Myra tuned right in to me. "You and Judy are gonna be best friends."

… Judy.

Chapter Six

Today was something called Monday, which meant tomorrow was not only something called Tuesday, it was the day Judy would come to take me back to my new home in Philadelphia. I was so excited I wagged my butt most of the day.

Myra could see how happy I was and smiled at me. "Tomorrow's the big day, Fella."

I know, I know, I know!!!

She patted me on my half-bald head. "You *know* tomorrow's Tuesday, don't you?!"

...Like the back of my paw.

Chapter Seven

I woke up Tuesday morning at the foot of Myra Glick's bed. She slipped into a pair of pink bedroom shoes, wrapped a robe around her pajama'd self, and then walked down the steps toward the kitchen.

"This is the last day we have breakfast together," she sighed.

I thought about how nice Myra had been to me. How compassionate she was to rescue me from that horrible mud pen situation. How she took me to her friend, Joel the Veterinarian, and then introduced me to lots of really great dogs at the shelter. Most of all, I thought about how she took me home with her and treated me with kindness and love and respect.

Myra Glick is a dog's best friend.

Just ask me.

While Miss Myra was drinking her coffee and I was finishing up the last of my Crunchy-Munchy Kibbles, her phone rang.

"Hi, Jude! I didn't think I'd hear from you until I was at work."

Myra laughed and again I listened intently to one half of the conversation.

"11:30 would be fine. ... What was that? ... Oh, that's such a cute name! I think it'll fit him just fine."

What name? She gave me a name?! I'm not gonna be called Boy and Fella anymore?

I thought back to my '800 kinds of dog' friend - you know, Sparky. Not that I didn't like the name Sparky; it was cute, and it fit him. But... I don't know, maybe with me being English and all that, I was hoping for something less cutesy - something a bit more dignified and British-sounding. Even if I did have blotchy skin, no hair, and sad eyes, I was still an Old English Sheepdog. My father came from champions, my mother was regal and beautiful. Yes, I deserved a proper name. Then I thought to myself, *What if Cedra and Ralph had given me a proper name, would it have mattered so much?*

No, it wouldn't.

I still would have been sad, lonely, sick, scared, and left to die.

So I shook all of those thoughts about a 'proper, dignified, English name' out of my unshaggy head. I didn't care if Judy called me Poopsie, Cutie-Pie, or Waggy Butt.

All I really wanted was for her to love me.

Chapter Eight

I sat in Myra's office, nibbling on a small dog biscuit. She looked down at me, gave me a pat on the head, and smiled, "It's 11:25, Fella! Your Mom'll be here any minute."

No sooner had those words left her mouth when Stella walked into the room. "Is your boy ready to go home? Judy's here!"

Judy's here!! I mean, my Mom's here!!

Myra stood up and attached a leather leash to the collar Joel the Veterinarian had placed on me the day I had left the mud pen.

I didn't want to appear too rambunctious, so I walked as calmly as I could, nervously leaning in toward Myra's legs.

"Don't worry," she said to me. "Everything's going to be just fine."

The front door of the shelter was only about twenty feet away. The old bloodhound barked to me, *"Good luck, there, Fella."*

"Thank you!" I barked back.

There were eleven dogs left in the shelter and they all wished me good luck, good health, and much happiness. Dogs are great, aren't they?

Only ten more feet to go.

Myra stopped and bent down to look into my eyes. "I'm sorry to see you go, Boy. But I know you'll be the happiest sheepdog in Philadelphia."

I kissed Myra on the face and again I wagged my butt.

Only five more feet to go.

Before I knew it, the front door to the shelter swung open and there she was. She ran right over to me. "You're soooooo BEAUTIFUL!!"

I'M beautiful?!

She wrapped her arms around me. "Oh, Henley! I'm so happy I'm gonna be your Mom!"

Henley?

"Do you like your new name? Myra, do you think he likes his name?"

Do I like it?!! It's perfect! It's English! ... Like Henley-on-Thames! Henley! My name is Henley! ... Henley, Henley, Henley! I love this woman already!

Judy sat on the ground and I snuggled into her lap. She looked up at Myra. "Isn't he adorable?"

"Well, Jude, I had a feeling the two of you would be a perfect fit for each other."

When Judy looked into my eyes, I took notice that hers were a soft blue, like Myra's. I guess I was just a sucker for a sweet woman with big blue eyes.

"Do I have any paperwork to sign?" Judy asked.

"I can send it to you. Don't even worry about it. You just take Old Henley Boy back home and get acquainted. I'm happy for both of you."

"Myra Glick, you're a dog's best friend," I heard Judy say. "Just ask me!"

Chapter Nine

The ride from Hoboken to Judy's home in Philadelphia took an hour and thirty-five minutes. It was the best ride of my life!

Myra had given Judy the blue and white blanket I had come to know and love, and Judy gave me a bright red dog collar with a matching leash. There was a beautiful brass nameplate attached to it in the shape of a bone.

It read:

Henley
215-555-1116

I was official!

Judy and I talked about lots of things on the ride home from Hoboken. She told me she had a nice house with a really big back yard and that we'd go for walks three times a day and that anytime she went out in the car, I could go with her.

I also found out that she was an editor and she worked at home, so we'd *always* be together. It doesn't get much better than that!

Judy was a happy soul and she played music for me as we drove toward my new home. They were an English band.

How appropriate.

Judy said they were called The Beatles.

It made me think back to some of the bugs I used to eat in my old mud pen days. But as soon as the music came on and she sang to me, long gone were the thoughts of those other beetles, and the only things I could think about were my new life, my happy new home, and the woman Myra had introduced to me as Judy, whom I would now and forever, call Mom.

I found myself wagging my English butt to the English beat.

…Hey Jude, don't make it bad, take a sad song, and make it better…

Chapter Ten

Life on Bainbridge Street was glorious. Every once in a while I'd think back to my Mother and Father, my eleven siblings, the old bloodhound, and Sparky, and I hoped with all of my heart that they had it even half as good as I did.

At the foot of Judy's bed was a huge, comfortable dog bed. It even had my name embroidered all over the top cushion: Henley... Henley... Henley... Henley. I felt lost in it sometimes, but then I'd realize that one of these days I wouldn't be a puppy. I'd be a grown up dog - a HUGE dog - hopefully as magnificent as my father. Then I'd really need a big bed!

Days turned into weeks, and weeks turned into months... my skin condition healed up, I started to put on weight, and my hair was growing like a weed. And, best of all, my Mom was crazy about me!

Judy's friends loved me too, and they were wonderful people: Monti and her daughter, Mallory, Francisco and Lou, Ruth, Lois, Betsy, Donna, Anna Marie... lotsa people. They'd all drop by and bring me treats, pat me on the head, and tell me I was adorable.

And of course, I was.

I didn't realize just how much my hair had grown or how big I was getting until the six-month anniversary of my birth. Judy picked me up and held me toward her dresser mirror.

"Happy sixth-month birthday, Henley! Look at you! You're gorgeous!"

I could hardly believe my eyes.

Inside my head I was still this skinny, mottle-skinned, sad-eyed, half-bald puppy, who only had personality to go on. But when my Mom held me up to that mirror, I almost reminded myself of my father. I had tripled in size and I had a full body of thick, gorgeous, Old English Sheepdog hair.

From that day on, I had a different kind of walk, a more dignified air. Not that I was full of myself; I wasn't about to forget where I came from. I was just doing my heritage proud.

Chapter Eleven

My first holiday season was the best!

On Christmas Day, Mom gave me a brand new Philadelphia Eagles leash and collar (we're both big fans), a dog slicker, a new set of nail clippers, two HUGE bones, and some really great treats made in England - of course.

During the holidays, I ate like a king. Not only did Mom slip me an extra treat or two, but Judy's friend, Monti, owned a restaurant on South Street, which was only a few blocks away, so Monti would often come over and bring me leftovers. Monti and Mallory also gave me a great gift for Christmas. I got a big, double dog bowl for water and food that sat up far off the ground, the same level as my head. It came wrapped in a big red bow.

I also got an Eagles jersey and a stuffed cat from Mom's son, Jon.

…More about cats later.

Mom was a hard worker, *especially* during the holidays. She'd stop and take a break from her writing work, but I noticed it was usually to do laundry, go Christmas shopping, reconnect with some friends, bake, clean, iron, or take me out somewhere.

She had a lot of holiday spirit, and everyone that came by our house just raved about the beautiful tree, her delicious home made cookies, and the wonderful time they had with us. I loved the whole atmosphere.

I was now part of a different kind of pack and I was one happy dog!

But then I noticed, as we loving dogs do, that maybe in all of my Mom's giving, somehow she was coming up short.

The night of her annual Christmas party, after everyone had left, she patted me on the head and wished me a Merry Christmas. I thought that was sweet. We walked up the steps and I sat outside the bathroom door listening to the shower water running. Soon Mom came out dressed in her warm flannel jammies and we both headed toward the bedroom. Mom snuggled under her down comforter, and I snuggled into my Henley bed, a bed that I would soon fill up entirely. I hoped that Mom had had a wonderful Christmas like I did and I think she did... but there was just *something* missing.

Chapter Twelve

After the New Year was celebrated, the time seemed to fly, and my first birthday was soon upon me.

Monti took a picture of me and Mom, which, as soon as it came back from the camera shop, went immediately on top of the fireplace. I couldn't get over how big I looked! Mom sent a copy of it to Myra. I thought that was really nice of her.

Now it appeared that I was no longer a puppy; I was officially a 'Dog.'

Yup, my one year mark gave me new status, and my days were filled with adventure. Mom would take me on nice long walks in two different dog parks in beautiful Center City Philadelphia.

I made friends with a Bull Mastiff named Lenny, a West Highland Terrier named Angus, and a mixed breed that reminded me of Sparky, named Jedi. We all had it pretty good.

"They're a proud lot, those sheepdogs," I heard Angus say as I walked toward the park exit.

"Indeed they are," Lenny answered.

One day, when Mom was walking me home down 5th Street, a stray dog dodged in-between two cars. One nearly hit him and Mom screamed.

"Come here, Fella. Come 'ere, come 'ere," she practically begged. Mom was trying her best to bring the dog to us because she knew he'd be safe.

The dog was scared. His tail was between his legs, he wasn't wearing a collar, he was dirty, and he looked awfully hungry.

My mind immediately went back to the farm and my mud pen days. I called out to him, *"Come on over here, brother! You'll be safe!"*

The dog turned around and looked back at me, *"I can't! People aren't safe! People are cruel!"*

He started to trot down the street, his pace quickening with each step.

"No! Not my Mom! She'll take good care of you!"

"I can't risk it. Listen, I… I gotta get outta here!" His head nervously turned from right to left. *"I can't stay, but thanks, big fella."* He turned away from me, ran across Rodman Street, and I never saw him again.

* * * * *

When Mom and I went home that day, I thought about the hungry, scared, and abused dog I had seen on 5th Street. I followed Mom around the house and watched her as she went about the rest of her day. I could tell she was thinking about him, too. We dogs are intuitive that way. But I didn't need any intuition at all to know that Judy was a good person and a great dog mom. She was kind to me, and pleasant to everyone she talked to… not that she didn't have her bad days, or her sad days; she did, but she was always very sweet to me – no matter what. And she would have been a great dog mom to that scared little fellow that ran across Rodman Street too, if she'd been given half a chance.

* * * * *

Mom and I were good company for each other. Sometimes we'd even watch TV together. Mom would actually let me up on the bed with her as she would watch a show or two in-between editing some work for a client. I thought that was great! I noticed that at the end of some of the programs there would be a public service announcement talking about a certain dog or cat who needed a home. Some shows were totally devoted to helping abused animals. Some were about how animals were being abused. I remember one that we watched. It was about some people who used their Pit Bulls to fight each other.

I know two Pit Bulls from my daily travels, Emma and Rollo. They are two of the nicest, most loving dogs you'd ever wanna meet. Then there were stories about carriage horses that lived in atrocious surroundings, puppies left to starve, and people with sixty-five cats, all of which were sick and neglected. What are their owners thinking?!

You know, you humans are an odd breed. You are gifted with so many wonderful things, you have

34

so many great opportunities, so many chances to improve your lives, to improve the lives of your fellow man, as well as your fellow animal friends. And yet most of you don't do anything about anything!

We don't ask much of you, you know. We really don't. I mean, I don't need dog treats from Great Britain, or an Eagles jersey. Any dog could live without that stuff. What we need is love. We need respect, some kindness. We are loyal and devoted companions. Yes, we are. We'll listen to your heartache, jump up and down with you when you're happy, and keep your feet warm at night, if you need it.

There's no need for millions of animals to be 'put down' or abused or neglected. No dog or cat or horse is responsible for that - only humans are.

When I go to sleep at night in my nice, soft bed, I *always* think about that stray dog on 5th Street. I pray that someone took him in and gave him a good home. I also pray that I'll never see another dog like him again. But that's just not realistic, given the nature of some human beings. Is it?

As Mom says, "The more I see of most people... the better I like my dog."

Chapter Thirteen

The Spring and Summer of 1999 were great. Mom got a house over in New Jersey with an even bigger yard, and I was in heaven. I tried to make friends with some of the squirrels and rabbits in our garden, but they wouldn't hear of it.

"You don't know what you're missing," I called after one floppy-eared bunny. *"I'd be a great friend!"*

The three pound rabbit couldn't be less interested in being friends with a sheepdog who now weighed over 85 pounds.

I coulda sworn I heard him say as he hopped over a tomato plant, *"You don't want me to be your friend... you want me to be your lunch!"*

With the warm weather upon us, Mom trekked to Philadelphia on a regular basis. I'd ride over there with her most of the time. I loved the car! I even had my own special seatbelt. And Mom's old BMW had a moon roof. Was *that* ever fun! It was situated so that when I rode in the back, I could stand up and hang my head out the roof and let that wonderful breeze rush all over my fuzzy face. What a great feeling! Kids would smile and wave at me and laugh. I guess it looked pretty funny, but I didn't care. I was with my Mom, the wind was whipping all around me, and I was taking in all the sites: The Ben Franklin Bridge, The New Jersey State Aquarium, Independence Hall... Sometimes we'd even take a ride down the shore. We'd always pull over at Farley's Rest Stop on the way down to Townsends Inlet, and Mom would get me a double burger (no fries) from the restaurant there. It was pretty good.

Not bad for a hairless puppy from an old mud pen, huh?

Chapter Fourteen

The days that I didn't ride over to Philadelphia with Mom were few. When she didn't take me along with her, it was usually later in the evening. My day was winding down anyway, so that was okay with me. I had my socializing in the daytime with Emma, Rollo, Angus, Lenny, and Jedi, so it was only fair that Mom had hers at night at Monti's restaurant. What a great place that was! It was even named after Monti. It was called MontSerrat. Even though Mom was gone for only an hour or two, she'd always bring me back a special treat. As I said before, Monti had great leftovers at her place. So, when Mom came home, I would have a nice big bag of huge steak bones and chicken filets to mix in with my Crunchy-Munchy Kibbles.

Again… not bad for a hairless puppy from an old mud pen.

One night in late August of 1999, Mom came home with my 'doggie-bag' and she said to me, "Oh, Henley… I met a wonderful man! You're gonna love him!"

A man?

Mom could tune me in like Myra used to. She patted my head and smiled, "Yep! An absolutely wonderful man, Hen! I think he's the one… which *could* mean you'll not only have a mom… you'll have a dad, too!"

I wagged my butt at the mere thought of it.

As Mom was mixing the 'beef tips au poivre' into my dog dish she added, "His name is Andrew."

Nice name.

"And he has a cat named Mandy."

I looked up from my bowl.

Did she just say…?

Chapter Fifteen

Soon Mom's wonderful man became a regular part of our household.

I liked Andrew. He'd play ball with me, take me for walks, and treat me to the occasional hamburger. What was not to like?

Mom and I would see Andrew every other week. He would fly up to visit us. I thought that was great! Here was a loyal and devoted human! Andrew lived in a place called Ft. Lauderdale, Florida. But he was originally a Philly area boy from a nice town called Yardley, so visiting us was more than just a visit. It was a trip home.

I always had such a good time with Andrew that I had forgotten all about what Mom had said to me a few months earlier, *"And he has a cat named Mandy."*

Over the course of a year and a half, Andrew flew up to visit us faithfully, twice a month. He also took all of his vacation time and sick leave time to spend with us.

Mom was never happier. Even her friends noticed that.

"This is the man I've waited for all of my life, Henley," she smiled at me as she dressed to pick up

Andrew at the airport. "I think the three of us should have a nice dinner at home. Whaddya think, Hen?"

I wagged my butt.

"Get your leash and let's get goin'."

Now, not only had I grown into a pretty impressive-looking sheepdog, I was a pretty smart one, too. I ran for my leash that was attached to the back door and pulled it right off its handle.

"COME ON, HEN!"

I galloped back into the living room, leash between my teeth.

"Good boy! Now let's go get your Dad!"

* * * * *

That weekend, the usual trips to Monti's restaurant didn't take place. Mom and Andrew were in the house all weekend with me, except for my usual walks in the park or a ride in the car to the grocery store.

I liked being around the two of them. They were a very loving couple and they truly enjoyed each other's company. I thought that was great! And better yet, that weekend they were making plans about their future. I heard the words, "leaving Ft. Lauderdale for good" … "getting married" … and "I hope he gets along with Mandy," more than once.

Andrew sat down on the sofa while mom was making some coffee. I hopped up next to him (I was allowed) and put my head in his lap.

Andrew reached into his wallet and pulled out a snapshot taken in his Florida apartment. "Look, Hen," he said. Andrew pointed to a cat that had nonchalantly walked into a picture being taken of himself and a few friends. "This is Mandy."

I sniffed the photo.

"See? She's black and white… like you are."

Actually, I'm more a dark charcoal gray.

"Mandy's never been around a dog before and she's seven and a half years old."

This could prove interesting.

I put my head back into his lap.

"She's very calm and serene."

Well, that's nice. I have the same disposition.

"I'm going to drive her up here right after the holidays. We can all live together."

Mom walked into the room and brought Andrew some coffee and a freshly made piece of chocolate layer cake.

I got a dog biscuit.

"Did you understand all that, Hen?"

Andrew smiled and thanked Mom. "Of course he did!"

Yeah, I got it. Mandy… a cat… seven and a half… calm and serene - like me.

Chapter Sixteen

"ANDREW!!! GRAB MANDY!!!!"

"I CAN'T!!! GRAB HENLEY!!!!!"

Needless to say, the day that Mandy and Andrew became a permanent part of our household wasn't as calm and serene as any of us had planned.

Mom welcomed Andrew with a very happy smile, a nice hug, and a big kiss. I jumped up and down, wagged my butt, and gave my dad a few kisses of my own.

A new day was dawning!

About five minutes after my dad settled in and the luggage was taken upstairs, he walked outside and then came back into the house with a very nice silver and white carrier of some kind, and inside of it... was Mandy.

This is a cat?

She just looked like a big fur ball to me. I didn't even growl. Mom held me back for a bit just the same, and then she sent me to the backyard while Mandy adjusted to her new surroundings.

I never left the back porch. I kept craning my neck to see what was going on. I think I even barked a few times, but no one paid any attention to me.

As I recall, Mandy was left sitting in the cage for about ten minutes before they let her out. She sat there sniffing, yawning, and making a few funny-looking faces.

Then, I heard Andrew say, "I'm gonna let her out, Jude."

Mom nodded an okay.

Andrew opened Mandy's cage, and she walked out of it like she owned the place. She was black and white, like they said, she didn't have a collar on, and she appeared totally unfazed by *everything*. I saw her nearing a big beef bone Mom had cooked for me. She sniffed it for a little while and then, when I saw her lift her head, she had a really weird look on her face, like she'd just smelled a pair of nasty, cheesy-smelling gym socks.

The nerve!

Mandy soon made herself comfortable on the arm of the sofa, and apparently that was the okay for me to come back into the house.

Mom came out to me, patted me on the head, and then she led me by the collar back into the living room. I wasn't in there for two seconds before Mandy puffed herself up, arched her back like one of those Halloween cats, and then took off for the kitchen.

Now, this is where those things called animal instincts and the word 'food-chain' come into play. I broke away from Mom so fast that she didn't know what hit her.

The house that we lived in had this weird floor plan where all the rooms opened up to one another, so I could run past the steps, into the kitchen, into the spare room, then into a little hallway, past the bathroom and a large bedroom and then back into the living room. One BIG circle!

Mandy ran through one room after the next, after the next, and I was running right after her.

One time around the house…

Two times around the house…

Three times around the house…

"ANDREW!!! GRAB MANDY!!!!"

"I CAN'T!!! GRAB HENLEY!!!!!"

Now, I'd never admit it back then, but cats are pretty smart animals.

By the time our fourth trip around the house came along, Mandy noticed there was a staircase. So, instead of running from the living room into the kitchen, as she had on three previous occasions, she ran from the living room right onto the third step from the bottom of the stairs and just sat there.

I kept running.

Four times around the house…

Five times around the house…

Six times around the house…

By the seventh spin I was losing steam and I noticed Mom and Dad were laughing like crazy. On my eighth trip I stopped, wondered where the cat was, and then walked over to the sofa.

Hey! What's goin' on?

Mom was still laughing when she hugged me. "Well, that's enough exercise for you today, Big Boy!"

Just then, out of the corner of my eye, I noticed a black tail swishing on the steps. I craned my neck once again and saw Mandy staring right at me.

"You're an idiot."

"I'm a what?!" I barked.

"You heard me."

She swished her tail once again and then leisurely walked up the staircase.

Chapter Seventeen

What a difference a few months make! Not that Mandy and I had become the best of friends, but at least we were tolerating each other.

Well, that's not quite true. Actually, I kinda liked her.

She was tolerating *me*.

"I'm hanging some clothes out on the line!" I heard Mom call out. "You two behave yourselves!"

I watched from the back door window as she carried her laundry basket to the clothesline. I wagged my butt, Mom smiled at me, and then I decided I'd go upstairs and chew on one of my dog bones for a while.

I sniffed around for a bit until I finally found the one I wanted. It was right where I had left it - under the sofa. I carried the bone up to Mom and Dad's bedroom, made myself comfortable on their nice oriental rug, and then proceeded to gnaw away.

"Must you make that racket?!"

I ignored the comment and continued to chew.

"Are you deaf?!" Mandy looked down at me from the bed where she was perched high atop two down pillows.

I stopped chewing. *"What's your problem?"* I didn't growl, but I did snarl at her a bit.

"Is that cute shaggy dog face supposed to scare me? Don't make me laugh."

I dropped my bone and sighed. *"Can't we just get along?"*

She gave me one of those 'looks', turned around in a circle three times, and then resituated herself on the pillows.

I started to chew again and then immediately thought the better of it. I grabbed the bone and was just about to head downstairs when she called to me once more.

"Henley?"

"What?"

"Remember when we first met?"

I turned to look at her. *"Yeah."*

"And I called you an idiot?"

"What about it?"

"Well, it was nothing personal, it was just that..."

"That what?"

"You're a dog."

"Nothing personal?!" I sat back down on the floor and started to chew that bone as loud as I could.

Mandy hopped off the bed and stood right next to me. *"Don't even think of growling! I don't want your stupid old bone... frankly, it stinks."*

"Is that so?"

"Yes, it is so. And, for your information, a cat's sense of smell is far superior to that of a dog."

I continued to chew.

"Henley."

"What now?"

"I've been watching you."

"Why?"

"It's what we do."

"And?"

"You waste too much energy. You're too available to humans. You're far too sociable, and you don't clean yourself properly."

"Is that right?" I said, still chewing.

Just then I heard the door open and Mom walked back into the house. "Henley! Mandy! Did you two behave yourselves?"

I got up, dropped the bone, and then started to head down the steps.

"See?" Mandy said, *"You'll go running to her but **she** will come to me! It's not a dog's world, Henley old boy… it belongs to the cats! Now, run along, Sheepdog."*

Mandy swished her tail in my face and then hopped back up on the bed.

"HENLEY! MANDY!"

I turned and looked at Mandy as she made herself comfortable. Then I ran down the stairs into the welcoming arms of my mother.

"How's my boy?!" she smiled as she patted me on the head.

I wagged my butt and gave her a few quick kisses on her face.

Then… she did it.

"Man-deeee? Where are you, Sweetie?"

I nudged her arm and acted all cutesy. She patted my head again. "Where's our Mandy girl, Hen?"

Our Mandy girl? ...Speak for yourself.

Mom started to walk up the steps.

"Mandy?"

I followed her.

"Miss Man-ners???"

I hate it when she calls her that.

"Where's Mommy's Boo-Boo Kitty?"

That's even worse.

Mom walked to the top of the steps and then turned into the bedroom.

There sat Her Royal Highness, just as I had left her, perched high atop two deliciously soft and comfy down pillows.

"There you are, Sweetheart!"

Mom walked over to her *precious Boo-Boo Kitty* and scratched her head, scratched under her chin, and then adjusted her pink rhinestone collar.

I sat down on the floor and sighed. Mom left the room and then Mandy turned toward me.

"I rest my case."

Chapter Eighteen

Aloofness only works for cats.

When a dog just sits around the house, wants to sleep all day long, and barely responds to his master, we don't get the doting cat treatment... *we* get taken to the vet! They think we're sick, that something has to be wrong with us. It's our diet, maybe we caught some kind of 'bug' from outside the house, or from another dog... Ugh.

Nope. We made our dog bed and... well, you know what I mean.

One edge I did have over Miss Man-ners was that I adjusted to her more easily than she adjusted to me. Maybe it was her need for this air of superiority, maybe it's just a 'cat thing', *or* maybe she really liked me and just enjoyed razzing me now and then. Actually, I think that was the real reason.

One morning after Dad left for work, Mom headed down the steps to straighten up the house. I decided to get up, go downstairs, and watch her. Just as I was moving toward the bedroom door, Mandy called to me.

"Where are you going?"

"What's it to you?"

"*Nothin' ... just asking.*"

I started to walk away again.

"*Are you coming back here any time soon?*"

"*Why? You gonna miss me?*"

She gave me that 'look', yawned, and then turned her back to me, "*Oh, puh-leeze.*"

Chapter Nineteen

If you think time flies when you're a human, try being a dog. Remember that 'one human year equals seven to a dog' thing? Do the math on that one!

But, I guess the most important thing was that Mandy, Mom, Dad, and I had a really nice life together. And as time moved on, things got even better. Miss Man-ners and I learned a lot about each other, and Mandy even trusted me enough to tell me that she was a rescued animal too.

"How'd that happen?!"

"Well, my owner, a darling of a woman, was moving to a new condo and they didn't allow any pets and..."

"Why was that?"

"Who knows. But, she had a very nice man as a neighbor and..."

"Andrew?"

"Of course, Andrew. She told him about her situation, and that if she couldn't find someone to take me, I'd end up back in the shelter where I started."

"So, then Andrew..."

"Well, of course he took me in."

"How old were you then?"

"Almost two."

"Were you ever at a puppy mill?"

She sighed. "Henley, I'm a cat. Why would I…"

"Oh. I get it… I get it…"

"So it took me a while to adjust to my new home. See, Andrew had another cat named Mason. Actually, Mason belonged to his roommate, Joe."

"Tell me about him."

"Joe?"

"No. Mason."

"Oh! Well, he was a Maine Coon and…"

"I thought you said he was a cat."

"He **was** a cat."

"But you just said he was a coon. Isn't that what they call raccoons?"

Again she sighed. "Of course that's what they call raccoons. But it's also the proper name for a certain breed of cat. You know, like you're a dog, but you're an Old English Sheepdog."

"Oh… I get it!"

She shook her head at me.

"Mandy?"

"What?"

"What breed are you?"

"Well, I'm not a…"

"Not a?"

"I'm not a true…"

"Not a true breed? So, you're just a… a mutt?"

I felt terrible after I said that.

Suddenly, Mandy puffed herself up. Not like the Halloween cat she was when I first met her, but puffed out like a proud and regal animal.

"I am what they call a Tuxedo Cat, for your information."

"Well. I..." (*Think fast, Henley.*)

"You what?"

"Well, I... I think Tuxedo Cats are the best! I mean, what do I know, I'm just a dog, but, in my opinion, I think they're the greatest, the most intelligent, and the..."

She almost smiled at me.

"You know," Mandy said as she was walking away, *"I actually think I like you."*

Chapter Twenty

Summer quickly rolled by... then there was another fall and another winter. Soon it was the year 2000, then it was 2001. Over that lengthy course of time, Mandy and I had become really good friends. We'd both sleep in the bedroom with Mom and Dad each night. Of course, I was in my Henley bed and Miss Man-ners was on the top of Dad's pillow, curled up over his head. And she purred! Did she ever purr! Talk about *dogs* making a lot of noise. HAH! This cat rattled like a bad car engine.

On the days that Mom would take me for a car ride, Mandy would sit sunning herself in the front window. Actually, I knew she was sitting there waiting for me to show up, but she used the sun as a cover up for her true feelings.

"Awww, how sweet. You missed me!" I said as Mom opened the front door.

"Don't flatter yourself. I'm a cat! We all sit in windows."

"Oh, puh-leeze," I sighed.

"Like it or not, I was just basking in the sunlight, Sheepdog."

"What?"

*"I was **sunning** myself! Nothing more... nothing less."*

"Okay, okay, burst my bubble. You weren't waiting for me." I walked away and headed for my water bowl.

Mandy followed me into the kitchen on her way to the basement.

"I'm happy to see you, Hen."

I never said a word. I just wagged my butt.

Chapter Twenty-One

Dad took off for a few days to spend time with Mom and me and Mandy. He was tired and he needed to 'recharge his batteries.' We were all happy to have him home with us.

His first day off was Monday. Mom and Dad slept in late. When they got up, they made breakfast: scrambled eggs, bacon, fried peppers and onions, hash browns, buttered rye toast, coffee, and freshly squeezed orange juice. They even scrambled a few eggs for me and Mandy!

They both hung around the house, played a game called Scrabble, took me for a walk, and then I rode with them over to the grocery store.

As for Mandy? She was just 'sunning' herself in the front window.

When we got back, Dad decided to call his family up in Mill Grove, Mom called Monti, and then they watched a special on PBS about Meerkats. Cute little things. Not as cute as me or Mandy… but cute.

We all ate lunch, Mom and Dad put on some CDs, and the two of them danced together in the kitchen. I thought that was sweet. Dinner time came and went, they played three more games of Scrabble, and soon it was time for bed.

"Night, Hen!"

"G'night, Mandy!"

Mom turned to Dad and said, "Goodnight, Sweet Prince."

And, as it was every night since they were together, Dad responded with, "Goodnight my beautiful Princess."

Then they gave each other a kiss, and soon we were all fast asleep.

And all was right with the world.

… But not for long.

Chapter Twenty-Two

Tuesday, September 11th, 2001.

"Andrew! MY GOD! Wake up!"

It was barely 9:00 AM.

The events of that day were shocking and the reports came rapidly, one right after the other:

8:45 AM: A hijacked passenger jet, American Airlines Flight 11 out of Boston, Massachusetts, crashed into the north tower of the World Trade Center. It tore a huge, gaping hole in the side of the building, sending thousands of pounds of debris flying down onto the streets. The building was hopelessly on fire.

9:03 AM: A second hijacked airliner, United Airlines Flight 175, again from Boston, crashed into the south tower of the World Trade Center and exploded on impact. Both buildings were now burning.

9:17 AM: The Federal Aviation Administration shut down all New York City area airports.

9:21 AM: The Port Authority of New York and New Jersey ordered all area bridges and tunnels closed.

The day went on and the news worsened.

American Flight 77 crashed into The Pentagon… Flight 93 crashed into a field in Somerset County, Pennsylvania…

Mom cried…
Dad cried…
The whole world cried.

Mandy and I just didn't get it. Dogs and cats are enemies by our very nature, you know the old saying, 'they fight like cats and dogs???' Yet, with patience and understanding, we have learned to co-exist, to be good friends, to be respectful of each other, and see things from a different point of view. And it's all good.

Just a thought here folks, but if dogs of all different sizes and colors, and cats of all different sizes and colors can get along… why can't you?

Chapter Twenty-Three

Sometimes people impress me to the point where I actually feel pride and hope in my heart for all of humanity.

After 9/11, America united. I noticed smiles appearing on people's faces more easily, and, in general, humans were kinder to each other as well as nicer to me and my fellow animal friends.

A tragedy of such monumental proportion shouldn't be what brings people together but, sometimes that's the way it happens.

I even noticed Mom and Dad giving more of themselves than usual. They were reaching out to help kids in bad situations, helping give a boost to the literacy program, and forming Teen Writers Guilds to bring kids together and to give them a voice.

Monti donated food, time, and clothing to a local soup kitchen, Mallory became an animal rights activist (and a Vegan)... Andrew's brother Bill joined his local Community Center to help those in need, Andrew's Mom and Dad gave Marriage Seminars at their church... The list was long and honorable.

I think all of these people realized that while a certain amount of life is about 'YOU', that doesn't translate into meaning that life is all about me-me-me! There's a BIG difference in all that.

When all you do is take and make demands for your 'rights', eventually you will build resentment and also drain a good many souls along the way... yourself included.

But when you learn to give back, the circle of goodness is never-ending.

Mandy and I were most fortunate to be a part of that kind of circle. And, even though we can't express it directly in words, except for here of course, our love and loyalty should speak volumes about our appreciation to those kind souls, like Mom, Dad, Myra, Mont, Mallory, Bill, Nan, Leon... who thought outside of themselves to make the world a better place than the way they found it.

Mom and Dad have a bumper sticker on the back of their car that says:

"Never believe that a few kind and caring souls cannot change the world, for indeed... that's all who ever have."

I say, it doesn't matter if you can find that bumper sticker and put it on your car or not. Just take those words and hold them in your heart and then go out into the world and bring them to life.

Your animal *and* people friends will thank you.

Chapter Twenty-Four

Soon another holiday season was upon us, and then another, and for the first time in a long while, Mandy and I heard the word 'marriage' come up in a conversation between Mom and Dad.

Christmas was their favorite time of year, and why not? There was joy, hope, happiness, the spirit of love and giving... So, appropriately, December 20th of 2002 was the date set aside for the official union of our wonderful, loving parents.

Mandy and I were thrilled!

The marriage was set in a local town hall that used to be a church. Andrew's family drove down from the mountains, some of Judy's family members arrived, and friends drove in from everywhere to celebrate the marriage of the two people Mandy and I loved most in the whole wide world.

There was a party at our house right after the wedding, and I was allowed to walk around and greet people. They'd pat me on the head and say "Hi!" and slip me a tiny piece of cake every now and then. I really loved all the attention... and the cake. Mandy stayed upstairs and slept, but... she's a cat... all that ruckus un-nerves her.

I walked upstairs carrying a cookie in my mouth that Monti had given to me.

"When are these people leaving?" Mandy said as she looked up from her cozy resting spot.

"I don't know. They're really having a good time."

"I'm happy for Dad and Mom."

"What?"

"I said I'm happy for them."

"That's not a very cat-like thing to say, is it?" I questioned.

"Probably not," she said as she curled her tail around her face, *"but I mean it with all of my heart."*

I was quite touched by my usually aloof friend's sentiment. *"Hey! Wanna share my cookie?"* I said as I dropped it on the bed right next to her.

"I don't think so, Hen. But thanks just the same."

"Too dog-like a gesture?"

"Umm, yeah… something like that."

"Well, Happy Wedding Day, Sister Mandy!"

"Yep. Happy Wedding Day, Brother Henley."

Chapter Twenty-Five

January 16th, 2003.

The phone rang, and once again I was privy to only one-half of the conversation.

"Hi. ... Really? ... Oh, geez, that's terrible! Two cats? ... Where are they again? ... I'll call Andrew."

Two cats?! What does this mean?

Mom hung up the phone and immediately dialed another number.

Again, I heard only part of what was going on, but I heard enough.

"Andrew, Mrs. Livingston called. ... Oh, it's so sad. ... A box full of cats, six of them, was left off at the pet store in Haddonfield. ... The note said they were born on December first. ... They're just babies. ... There's only two left, and... Yes, isn't that a shame. ... Sisters. ... Can we?! ... Really?! ... Oh, she'll have such a good home here and..."

That was all I needed to hear. I bypassed the bone I had been chewing on and walked up the steps to see Mandy.

I entered the bedroom.

"Wake up."

"Go away."

"Okay, I'll go away and then you can just be surprised when your Dad brings home a kitten tonight. See ya!" I turned to head back down the staircase.

Mandy jumped off the bed and stood next to me.

"What are you talking about?"

I explained as much of the conversation as I possibly could and then added that the new addition was a rescue animal just like we were.

"Rescue, schmescue! It's a kitten!"

"So?"

"A kitten! Young… cute…"

I could sense a feeling of loss in Mandy, you know, that she wouldn't be top dog anymore. No pun intended.

She was worried that the cute little kitty would get all the cat-type love and affection that had always been totally reserved for her. For the first time since I knew her, Mandy looked forlorn. I sat down on the rug right next to her.

"Mandy."

"What?"

"Mom and Dad are doing a good thing."

"Yeah, I guess."

"And you know what?"

"What?"

"You're still the Queen of the House. You always will be. No one could ever replace you."

"Henley."

"What is it?"

"Say that again."

"Say what again?"

"*The Queen thing.*"

"*Oh! Well, you're still the Queen of the House. You always will be. No one could ever replace you! Not ever! No way!*"

Mandy sighed, hopped back on the bed, and then made herself comfortable.

"*It'll be nice to have a little kitty in the house… won't it, Hen?*"

Chapter Twenty-Six

For the first time in a long time, Mom left the house and drove away in the car without me. From what I heard of another quick conversation on her cell phone, Mom was going to meet Dad and then head to the pet store where they would pick up the newest member of our household.

Mandy walked downstairs, grabbed a bite to eat, took a drink of water, and then hopped up into the window and stared out into the darkness.

"Waiting for someone or just 'sunning yourself'?"

"Very funny."

She hopped off the window ledge and then started to walk up the staircase.

"Let me know when the little darling arrives."

I turned toward her from the position I had manned at the side window. *"I will."*

One set of headlights after another drove down our street, but still no Mom and Dad.

Where are they?!

No sooner did that thought leave my head than Mom and Dad pulled into the driveway. I watched Mom exit from the side door and Dad from the driver's side. He then opened the back door and took out Mandy's old silver and white carrier, and then the two of them were heading toward the house.

This is exciting!

I guess they figured I would be safe with a new kitten because I was now a 'cat-friendly' dog. So, rather than go through the routine I did when Mandy came up from Florida, they opened the door to the cat container immediately.

Out stepped a darling little black and grey and white kitten just about the size of a large dog biscuit.

"Well, aren't you sweet," I said as I walked over to her.

Immediately the kitten, who had no fear of my 110-pound shaggy self, scampered over to me and snuggled her face into my paw.

"We named her Cynthia." Dad smiled.

Cynthia… a nice British-sounding name.

I rested on the floor and my newest cat friend cuddled right up in-between my chin and my chest.

She didn't actually say anything to me, but she did purr.

Cute.

"And this is Rose!" Mom announced as another dog biscuit-sized kittie strolled out of the container.

Two cats!

"We couldn't leave with just one," Dad explained. "They were the only two left and…"

Mom finished his sentence, "They're sisters!"

Rose snuggled into me right next to Cynthia, and then the two of them started to play. They left my side and romped and jumped all over the place like two Mexican jumping beans.

I decided to leave Mom and Dad alone with the kitties and break the news, ever so gently, to Miss Man-ners.

As I entered the room, she lifted her head.

"Well? Is she here?"

"It's more like **they** *are here."*

"They?!"

"Cynthia and Rose."

"What?"

"Two kittens. They're sisters."

Mandy closed her eyes. *"Double trouble."*

I turned my head left and then right. *"Excuse me, but what did the* **Queen** *of the House just say?"*

She hopped off the bed.

"I said, 'Let's go down and have a look at the little darlings.'"

Chapter Twenty-Seven

Well, whether she liked it or not, the kittens were just crazy about Mandy.

They followed her everywhere.

I walked down to the basement, and Miss Manners had just chased Cynthia and Rose back up the steps.

"You know," I said as I walked toward her, *"You don't have to be bothered with the kittens if you don't want to. I can take care of them."*

She turned to look at me. *"You've got to be kidding."*

"No, seriously. I can teach them how to bathe themselves. I've watched how you do it. I can show them how to..."

"You're a dog!"

"I know. But we're pack animals. They'll be part of my pack!"

Rose and Cynthia were now sitting on the top step, listening to us.

"Does this mean we're gonna be dogs?" Cynthia's voice squeaked.

"It most certainly does not!" Mandy did her famous tail-swishing act right in my face and then she walked up the staircase toward the kittens. *"Come on, girls. Follow me. You've got lots to learn!"*

"*But what about* me*?!*" I felt so out of the loop.

"*You're a dog, Hen!*" Mandy turned, and Rose walked along right behind her.

Cynthia hopped down two steps and looked me straight in the eye. "*But you're a r-e-a-l-l-y nice dog!*"

Chapter Twenty-Eight

Mandy had the maternal thing down to a science. She never had any kittens of her own because she was 'fixed' like I was, but she was very kind and loving toward Rose and Cynthia just the same.

Rose was a striking cat in the looks department. She had long gray hair that almost looked a bluish-purple in a certain light, and she had these big orange eyes.

She was a quick study, and as soon as Mandy had taught her the basics, she was pretty much her own girl, so to speak. Rose would be cuddly when she was in the mood for it, but for the most part, she was true to her feline roots and she was independent, and quite the sleeper and sunbather.

Cynthia was very different. It amazed me how two sisters could look and act so unalike. Well, she did have the same long hair, but Cynthia was striped: gray, black, and white, and she had big greenish-yellow eyes. She was also far less aloof than 'Miss Rose'. Cynthia had more than one nickname, and for all the right reasons. She was called 'Flopsy Kitty' because every time she'd hop up on the sofa next to someone (for attention, of course) she'd flop right over on her back and kinda roll around like a dog. I guess that was the reason for her other nickname, 'Puppy Cat.'

Cynthia took a liking to me from the get-go. Mandy gave her all the 'do this' and 'do that' instructions, but I'd always catch her watching me for some reason. And when Mom and Dad would come into the house, all four of us would hear them, but being a dog, I was the only one to ever greet them, until one day, when I heard them call out, "We're home!" and as I started down the steps, I noticed that Cynthia was right behind me. Now it's an everyday thing. The Sheepdog and the Puppy Cat are the official house greeters! Cynthia also decided she would rather drink out of my water bowl than the cat's bowl, and so we share my water. There are even times, and I know this must sound strange, but when I'm eating my breakfast, or lunch, there's Cynthia, standing up on my bowl, having a drink right next to me.

Mandy gives her one of those 'looks', and so does Miss Rose, but Cynthia and I don't pay those two any attention. We're too busy having fun together.

Cynthia also decided she would take her naps with me, and so, when I curl up in my 'Henley bed', Cynthia hops right in with me and sleeps in-between my front paws.

"You're nice and warm, Henley!"

"Well, I've got a lot of hair, so I guess it's to be expected."

"Thanks for being such a nice friend." She yawned as her eyes started to close.

"Don't mention it, Puppy Cat."

* * * * *

One evening, I decided I would sleep in the guest room on the nice, soft Oriental rug Mom and Dad have in there. The last thing I remember before dozing off was Cynthia snuggling up next to me.

"Night, Hen."

"G'night, Cyn."

I guess it was one of those mornings when I was a light sleeper and I heard Dad's alarm go off. It was just about 5:00 AM.

I knew Dad would head for the shower and Mom would walk down to the kitchen to make some coffee, so I thought I'd go upstairs and greet them before they got out of bed.

As I started to get up, I noticed that not only was Cynthia snuggled up next to me, but so was Rose, and... so was Mandy!

I decided not to disturb any of them, and I lay back down on the rug. It was a nice feeling. I had a pack again: a sweet, kind, and loving pack. It reminded me of those days when I was with my mother and father and nine brothers and two sisters - those days before we were taken to Cedra and Ralph's mud pen. We would all snuggle together - soft, warm, comfortable, and safe. I thought about my mom and dad and wondered where they were. I also thought about my brothers and sisters. I hoped that they all had good homes like I did. I also hoped that they felt as loved and were as well cared for as I was. And, as I looked around at my three feline pack members, I also hoped that my old sheepdog family all had really nice friends.

... like I did.

Chapter Twenty-Nine

I overheard Mom talking to Dad about a weekend trip to the mountains to visit Dad's family. It appeared that it was going to be a three-day trip for just the two of them, so that meant we would spend the weekend at home with Mom's son, Jon.

Jonny really liked me. He would play roughhouse, run me around the backyard, and give me treats, and I'd watch him play video games on the big screen TV in the basement.

Jon also took a liking to all of the cats, and even though he was never raised with cats as a child, he became quite fond of them, and they liked Jon, too.

Right after breakfast, real early on a Friday, Dad and Mom said a goodbye to all of us. We got patted and brushed and hugged, we got treats, and of course, they told all of us they loved us and that they'd be back late Sunday evening. As soon as the front door closed and Mom and Dad headed for their car it was business as usual for Mandy, Cynthia, and Rose. And me? I had some problems with separation anxiety. I stood by the window and watched their car until it faded away into the scenery.

Jon immediately picked up on my mood.

"They'll be back before you know it, Hen. Hey, wanna go for a ride?"

The word 'ride' always triggered something magical deep within me, and as soon as that word left his lips, I ran to the door and grabbed my leash. Less than five minutes after Mom and Dad had left, Jon and I were barreling down the highway on our way to the local Seven-Eleven. Jon always got the same order: beef jerky, wasabi peas, and Gatorade.

And, bless his heart, he always got me a box of super meaty, extra crunchy, tasty, yummy, flavorful doggie snacks – the extra jumbo-sized box.

As I said, Jon really liked me.

Chapter Thirty

I was the first one to notice the headlights shining in our driveway.

I barked and Jon yelled to me, "Are they home, Hen?"

The cats were all sleeping upstairs, and all of my ruckus didn't change their status – but something soon would!

Mom was the first one in the door, and I ran around and acted like a goofy puppy because I was just so happy to see her. I ran into the dining room and grabbed my big dog bone and dropped it at her feet. Mom gave me a hug, and then Dad walked in the door, and I did my routine all over again, including dropping the bone at his feet.

Jon walked upstairs and they all greeted each other. I had a feeling something was going on because of the unusual smile on Mom's face.

Dad placed their suitcase in the guest room and then headed back out to the car.

"Wait 'til you see what we got, Henley!"

Jon smiled at me, followed Dad outside, and then closed the front door just about half-way.

I hope it's some super meaty, extra crunchy, tasty, yummy, flavorful doggie snacks in the extra jumbo-sized box and not...

"Two more cats!" Dad beamed as he walked back into the house holding a large carton close to his chest.

I immediately turned toward the staircase and there sat Mandy, Cynthia, and Miss Rose.

Cynthia ran down the stairs. *"Two more cats!"*

Rose walked down to the bottom step and sniffed the air. *"Kittens."*

Mandy never left her seat. She just sat there and stared at me. *"Did he just say two more cats?"*

I looked back at the large cardboard box and then back at Mandy.

"He sure did."

She turned and walked slowly back up the staircase. *"I'm gettin' too old for this."*

Chapter Thirty-One

The kittens were two little boys. They were named Mookie and Ned.

As soon as Dad put the carton down on the floor, Cynthia and Rose sniffed them and hissed a bit, but soon the four of them were scampering around and playing together as if they had been friends all of their lives.

As for Mandy, she decided to hide somewhere, away from all the ruckus. I don't remember seeing her for hours on end as the kittens frolicked from one end of the house to the other.

I stayed with my 'people pack' to find out exactly how we got to add two new cats to the family. Dad and Mom were talking to Jon about their trip and how it all came about.

I guess I shoulda seen this one coming.

See, my Dad's family lives in a beautiful part of Pennsylvania up in the mountains. Most people up there aren't farmers anymore, but they do love their land and they have some farm animals, maybe chickens, turkeys, some sheep… They grow some tomatoes and corn for their own use, and cats and dogs are everywhere! In the city, people are always reminded to spay and neuter their pets to cut down on unwanted animals. But farmers see their pets differently: cats chase mice out of those big old farmhouses, dogs herd, dogs go hunting. People don't mind if they have six or seven animals. It's part of farm life. But also part of farm life is losing animals to wolves, coyotes, and the occasional fast driver in a pickup truck.

Dad's sister, Laura, had some wild cats come and visit her when she moved in, and they never left. She would feed them and put fresh water out for them on her big front porch, and they loved her. Laura's husband, Doug, loved the cats too, and so did their children, Molly and Ian. They even named them: Poofy, Elsie, Cally, Scaredy Cat, Tiger, Brownie, Timmy, and Bob.

Molly wanted to keep all of the cats inside the house, but Doug and Laura already had two indoor dogs, Myles and Murphy, and two indoor cats, Razz and Lilly.

The 'outside' mommy cat, Poofy, kept having kittens, and Doug and Laura thought it would be best for the mom cat to be fixed and then to get all of her kids fixed too. Seven cats can become thousands of cats in less than ten years. That wouldn't be a good thing for the farmers or the cats.

The vet couldn't spay Poofy or her latest litter because it was way too early for all of them. But they took all the rest of the cats to their local veterinarian at The Animal Care Center in Danville. And, at a reduced fee, because Doug and Laura were good enough to do this, The Center made sure all of those cats had their shots and that they were fixed so that no one would have to worry about kittens that needed a home or kittens whose parents had disappeared for one reason or another.

Now, all was well with the cat world in Mill Grove, Pennsylvania.

… Thanks to Doug and Laura.

Right before Mom and Dad drove up to visit their family, Poofy and two of the kittens were among the missing. No one had seen them for over a week. After a few days Doug, Laura, Molly, and Ian, went looking for them, but not one of the three could be found. Just as they had given up hope for the missing mom and kittens, one of the baby cats came crawling onto their porch. She was so scared. She had bugs crawling in her blood-drenched hair, and half of her tail was missing. It was hard to tell if it was because of a trap, a car, or an animal attack. They took the kitten to The Animal Care Center, but it was too late. They figured that possibly Poofy had died while trying to save that kitten from a large, hungry animal. We can only guess what happened to the other kitty. That wasn't the end of the family's worries, though. There were still two kittens the mommy cat had left behind. They were living under the front porch of the house.

Now, humans have a phrase that goes: "Timing is everything," and so, those two kittens left under the porch, the ones that Ian and Molly had originally named 'Latté' and 'Peanut,' were part of some very perfect timing, and the two of them became the newest members of our loving household, now under the names, Mookie and Ned.

As time went on and the boys felt more comfortable at home with all of us, I'd hear the two of them telling stories of life on the farm to the three city cats in the house.

"Our Mom was a good hunter and she'd bring us mice to eat."

"Mice?"

"Yeah, they run around in the field and in the barn!"

"Run around?!"

"Sure they run. They have four legs like us, just that they're smaller and…"

"Wow! And your Mom was fast enough to catch them?!"

"She sure was."

"And we drank water out of the creek behind the house."

"That sounds like fun!"

"And sometimes I'd catch myself a bug or two right there in the grass, even when I was still a baby."

"Gee," Cynthia sighed. *"Well, sometimes I see a fly now and then outside of the house."*

"Huh?"

"And I see birds and squirrels and bunnies, but I never get to catch them."

"Why not?"

"Because we're housecats."

"Just housecats?!"

"That's us!"

"You mean we're never going to be able to go outside again?!!!"

Mandy interrupted, *"You boys will have a beautiful life here. You can sun yourselves safely, there will be no worries about cars running you over or people grabbing you and being mean to you… you'll be cool in the summertime and warm in the winter, you'll have a soft, comfortable bed, good fresh food and water, you'll get car rides now and then to see a doctor to make sure you're healthy, and you'll have people who will love you and cherish you for all of your life."*

"And," added Rose, *"We'll all have each other."*

"And," said the Puppy Cat, *"We'll all have Henley to look after us. Like a big fuzzy Nanny!"*

Mookie hopped up onto a nice, soft sofa cushion. *"Actually, I think we're gonna like being housecats!"*

Chapter Thirty-Two

It was now 2004 and the West family was complete. Dad, Mom, Mandy, Cynthia, Rose, Ned, Mookie, - and, of course... me.

Had Mom and Dad not rescued the six of us, we would have all had very short and scary lives.

Rose and Cynthia were found in a dirty oil-soaked box with no food or water on Federal Street in Camden, New Jersey. Dad took Mandy in when her owner could no longer keep her, and our boys, Ned and Mookie, never knew their father, and they lost their mom and only other siblings in what appeared to be some kind of horribly brutal attack.

And, of course, you know what happened to me back in my mud pen days.

We are all very lucky now and we know it.

We often talk about how we wished more families would adopt an animal now living in a shelter somewhere. You know, those sweet, sad faces, just longing for the day to become part of a kind, loving, and compassionate household. It breaks my heart just thinking about it. The shelter people are really wonderful souls. I know that from my own personal experience, but we all really want to belong to a family. I'm sure you can understand that.

Many of the dogs I meet in the park or in the neighborhood are also rescued dogs – like I was. We talk to each other about our old lives while our Moms and Dads are also chatting about us. Tiki was one of my newest friends. He was a big boy. He was almost my size. Tiki had short, dark hair, one blue eye and one brown eye, and he wore a red bandana around his neck. His family adopted him from the local shelter. He was found running on the street, no collar, hungry and scared, like that poor dog I met on 5th Street in Philadelphia. Tiki's original family got him for Christmas, but when the cute little puppy turned into a BIG dog, they didn't want him any longer; he was 'too much work.' So, they opened the door and just let him go. Tiki told me he stayed by the back door and cried for a few nights, but the family never let him back in again. He ran away looking for food, water, and someone to love him. He was rescued by a local SPCA volunteer who found him rummaging through her trash can for something to eat. Luckily for Tiki, a nice couple decided to look for a dog at that helper's nearby SPCA. He has had a wonderful, loving home ever since.

Another one of my friends is a sweet, graceful greyhound named Alice. Poor Alice.

Alice was rescued from a racetrack in South Florida. She now lives in a very happy home, and she has three cats as friends, too! Here's what Alice told me about greyhounds. People race greyhounds at racing tracks. People bet on the dogs and hope their dog wins. The dogs live in cages all of their lives and rarely have any happy and friendly human contact. The dogs are used to make money, and then, when they are injured or not fast enough anymore, they are killed. Alice was one of the lucky ones. In 2000, the year that Alice was rescued, about 19,000 greyhounds were killed. Can you imagine that?! And this includes 7,600 sweet little greyhound puppies who were farm culls (you know, rejected like I was, because I wasn't good enough), and another 11,400 'retirees' who weren't rescued. Alice's parents and all of her brothers and sisters were killed. Alice's aunt and uncle, and a few cousins, like many other greyhounds, were sold to research labs, or returned to breeding facilities to serve as breeding stock, or, worse yet, sent to racetracks in foreign countries where the conditions in which these sweet dogs have to live are just horrible… even worse than the mud pen where I came from!

It makes me sad just to think about it.

Chapter Thirty-Three

As I mentioned earlier, in 2004 our family was complete. And we really had a great time together. I found out that Mookie was the runt of his family too, and when he was born, his mother didn't even want to feed him because she thought he would die anyway. Then, his Mom moved all of her kittens from a hay-strewn cubby hole in the basement to underneath the large front porch... all but Mookie, that is. Doug and Laura and the kids watched the mommy cat carry one baby at a time up the stone steps directly to their new destination.

Molly was the one who immediately noticed that she carried only three kittens out to their new home. Shortly after she situated her babies, the mommy cat left for a trip to the woods to find some food, and Molly ran back to the basement and found 'Peanut', as Mookie was called at the time, all alone and crying. He was so much smaller than his siblings, and so skinny. Molly took him and put him under the front porch with the other kittens. For some reason, his mom took good care of him after that. Lucky for all of us that Molly had her thinking cap on, because that's what saved our Mookie Boy's life.

Chapter Thirty-Four

Now there were four kittens in our happy home. They were running Mandy ragged, but I know she loved it. They would follow her around like ladies-in-waiting follow The Queen.

Dad bought some toys from the local Pet Smart store, "for all the kids", and they really enjoyed them. Mandy had a favorite yellow ball with a bell inside of it that she'd swat around, Miss Rose liked fake, furry mice, Ned liked to climb on the cat stand and play with a ball that hung from the top of it like a punching bag, and Mookie was a smart and inquisitive cat who would do just about anything to create some excitement for himself, which included stealing all the other cats' toys, sliding down the steps like a 1950s 'Slinky' toy, and sitting in the bathroom sink trying his best to turn on the water faucet. As for my Puppy Cat? She liked bottle caps.

* * * * *

Mom and Dad took very good care of us. We went to the vet to get our shots. They would play with us. We would get bathed and brushed. We just loved their company so much. When they were in the living room, we would all end up in there and we'd just sit around watching them. Then, if they got up to go to their bedroom, well, then we'd all march up the steps and make ourselves comfortable there, too. It was a nice feeling to be around them, and so we were around them as much as possible.

This brings me to Christmas of 2004.

Mom and Dad bought a beautiful Scotch Pine tree for the holidays and we all sat in the living room and watched them decorate it. There were hundreds of sparkling white lights, all kinds of beautiful ornaments, and row after row of shiny silver beads.

Mookie seemed the most interested.

"Wow! That's some tree. I never saw one like that up in Mill Grove!"

"Well, this is a Christmas tree, it only happens once a year. Pretty cool, huh?"

"Yeah, look how sparkly it is!"

"Don't get any funny ideas," I warned him.

"Whaddya mean?"

"You know what I mean!"

About two hours later, the tree was completely decorated. The lights in the house were all turned off; just the Christmas tree was left to sparkle and shine. It was amazing! Cats don't seem dazzled by much, but even Mandy had to say something about that beautiful Scotch Pine.

"That's the prettiest tree I've ever seen."

"Gettin' sentimental in your old age?"

"No. It's just a fact. Nothing sentimental."

I watched as she turned away from me and headed up the front staircase.

I saw her stop and turn around to look at the tree one more time.

"She's an old softie," I whispered to my Puppy Cat.

"She is. But don't tell her you heard that from me!"

Mom and Dad eventually decided to go to bed, leaving the tree lights on to give the house some holiday spirit.

One by one we all headed upstairs and took our usual places, me in my Henley bed, Mandy curled up next to Dad, Rose resting next to his pillow, Ned snuggled beside Mom's knees, Cynthia in-between my paws, and Mookie…

Mookie?

Where's Mookie?!!

Chapter Thirty-Five

CRASH!!!!!!
BANG!!!!!!
BOOM!!!!

"What in heaven's name?!!"

I sprang from the bed to see what was the matter (that's a Christmas pun.)

Dad, Mom, Mandy, Rose, Ned, Cynthia, and I quickly ran out of the bedroom and down the front staircase.

"Good grief!" Mom put her hands up toward the side of her face as she surveyed the disaster.

"Now *who* could have done this?!" Dad said, turning toward Mookie, who just also happened to be surveying the disaster.

The rest of us stood on the steps and stared at him while Mom and Dad started the clean-up process.

"Mookie! What did you do?!" Mandy scolded.

"Hey, it was just one shiny ball and…"

"Well, you'd best see what you can do to make amends, young fella! One shiny ball indeed!" With that said, Mandy walked back upstairs. Rose followed, never saying a word.

Cynthia started back to bed along with Mandy and Rose but then turned toward him and said, *"Was it fun, Mook? It sure looks like it was fun!"*

I gave Mookie the evil eye to discourage him from recruiting the Puppy Cat for a future Scotch Pine debacle.

"Was it, Mook? Was it fun?"

"Come on, Cynthia!" I woofed.

"Was it fun? Huh?"

"Yeah," I heard Mookie whisper. *"It was awesome!"*

Chapter Thirty-Six

Christmas time was glorious! The house was filled with the wonderful smell of freshly-baked cookies, roasted turkey, and one very well-secured Scotch Pine Christmas Tree.

Family and friends filled our home, and we reveled in the beautiful holiday season. Mom would sing Christmas carols while she cooked, Dad would come home from work and put another gift under the tree every night, and it snowed! Man, did it snow! Mookie and Ned had never seen snow before and they were glued to the windowsill, never wanting to miss a moment of the magnificent show that Jack Frost was putting on for them.

Mom and Dad went outside to make a snowman in the back yard. We all watched from the window through one stage of design or the other. The cats got bored after a while, but I hung around and watched the activity. Mom came back in the house for one of her woolen scarves and one of Dad's, and then our Dad came in and took a few pieces of charcoal from the basement.

Then...

Voila!

I called to my feline friends, *"You should get down here and look out the window!"*

In the wink of an eye, Mookie came barreling down the steps, quickly followed by Miss Rose, Mandy, Ned, and the Puppy Cat.

"Well, will you look at that!" I heard Mookie say.

Mom and Dad saw all of us staring out the window.

I heard Dad call out, "HEY, GUYS! WHAT DO YOU THINK?!"

Truthfully, we all thought it was pretty awesome.

Not only had they made a snowman, but a snow-woman too. And right next to them?

Five snow cats and a big snow dog!

Now THAT, my friend, is talent!

Chapter Thirty-Seven

Before we knew it, another New Year was upon us. Mom and Dad passed on several invitations to attend local parties as well as a huge gala over in Philadelphia. They just wanted to stay home and be together to ring in the New Year. Mom made a nice dinner; they turned the tree lights on and then snuggled on the couch. All six of us were sitting around them. Mandy on top of the sofa ledge, Rose on one arm of the sofa, Cynthia on the other, Ned in Dad's lap, me at Mom's feet, and Mookie…

Mookie?

Where's Mookie?!!

I turned and spied him under the Christmas tree swatting at one of the ornaments.

"Haven't you learned your lesson by now?"

"Sorry, Henley." Mookie walked out from under the tree and snuggled up next to me.

"Happy New Year, Hen."

"Happy New Year, Mook."

Chapter Thirty-Eight

2005 was another great year! We moved to a bigger house with a really nice, fenced-in backyard. Dad put window hammocks upstairs for the cats to have a comfortable place to sit while they watched what was going on outside. I took three trips to the mountains with Mom and Dad, we went down the shore, and there were birthday parties and other happy celebrations. I took notice to the phone calls that Mom and Dad would get now and then, and as usual, although I could only hear part of the conversation, I knew exactly what was going on.

"Really, Ruth? ... How old is the dog? ... Okay. ... Does he have all of his shots? ... He's been neutered? I'll make a few calls and see if we can get the little fella a good home."

Then Dad:

"Where did they find the cat? ... Geez. ... That's a shame. Is she okay now? ... Well, that's great! ... All right, let me see if we can find her a nice home. ... I'll call you back as soon as I hear something."

My parents are good people. They work long, hard hours, but they still managed to find the time to help stray dogs and cats secure a loving home.

Mom and Dad's other animal loving friends would drop by and constantly marvel at the fact that I, a 110-pound sheepdog, could get along so well with five cats who, if you added their weight up together, didn't amount to one-third of me.

But it was true. We really liked each other. We'd take our naps together, play on the floor together, share a water bowl, and they would all sniff me when I came in from outside. You know, all those outdoorsy smells that they didn't get to experience the full effect of since they were all house cats. I guess you can only smell so much from an open window.

"Wow! That smells like a possum."

Cynthia was curious. *"How can you tell that, Mook?"*

"I remember it from the farm."

"Gee, Henley. Did you see a possum out in the yard today?"

"Not that I can recall."

"And you smell like a bunny, too!"

"Mookie remembers all the smells," Ned proudly announced.

"Farm instincts," Mookie stated.

"Did you see a bunny today, Hen?"

"Not today, but I have. They don't care too much for me."

"Why's that?"

"I think I scare them."

"You?!!" Mandy almost laughed. *"You are the sweetest animal in the whole world! That rabbit should have its head examined."*

Everyone (including me) was so surprised that Mandy would make such a loving statement. Not that she wasn't a darling of a cat, but she was always very uptight about showing her feelings and emotions.

"You think I'm sweet?!"

"Henley," she said as she walked away. *"I think you're the absolute best!"*

See what I mean about 2005 being a great year?!

Chapter Thirty-Nine
(Time marches on)

"You're gonna be eight years old this month, Hen! Can you believe that?!"

Mom flipped her calendar and there, marked right on March 10th, 2006, was a red heart with the name Henley inside of it.

How thoughtful!

"And Rose and Cynthia will be four on December 1st, and Mookie and Ned will be two on April 8th."

I looked at her and turned my head from right to left.

"Oh… you wanna know about Mandy, huh?"

She's always on my wavelength.

"Well, you know we always celebrate her birthday on May 11th, but truthfully, Andrew never knew when she was born, and neither did the lady who gave her to him. Originally, Mandy came from a shelter, so no one ever really knew what day she was born, who her parents were… nothing. They even guessed at her age."

Poor Mandy. Every one of us has a real birth date but her.

"So on May 11th, according to the way we've celebrated in the past, Mandy will be fourteen this year."

She's gettin' up there.

"She's a sweetheart, Hen. Like you."

She's more than a sweetheart. She's my best friend.

Chapter Forty

My March birthday was celebrated with some sheepdog treats, a deluxe hamburger (no cheese) and a box of super meaty, extra crunchy, tasty, yummy, flavorful doggie snacks – the extra jumbo-sized box.

Mandy was the first of my feline friends to wish me a Happy Birthday.

"Happy Birthday, Hen! Eight years old, already. Time flies."

"Yeah. I'm gettin' old."

"You?! I'll be fourteen on May 11th!"

"You're still a kitten! Remember Dad said he had a cat named Christine? She lived to be twenty-one!"

"That's true. Hey…"

"What?"

"How long do they say sheepdogs usually…"

"Live?"

"Yes."

"Around ten."

"Well, you're still a puppy! Remember Mom had a sheepdog named Winston? He lived to be fourteen!"

Mandy and I didn't like to talk numbers. We were both 'gettin' up there', and the thought of one of us without the other was just heartbreaking, so we always made the best of our time together, just in case…

Soon Mookie and Ned celebrated their second birthday with some new toys, tuna-flavored crunchy treats, and some catnip.

"Two years old… just babies," Mandy said to me.

… Then, it was May 11th.

The day Miss Man-ners turned fourteen.

That's about seventy-two in 'people years.'

Mandy didn't play with toys these days, and her teeth were wearing down, so tuna-flavored crunchy treats were out of the question. But Mom and Dad did give her a nice piece of Alaskan Salmon from mom's favorite super market, and she absolutely loved it.

"Happy Birthday, Mandy."

"Thanks, Hen."

Chapter Forty-One

The Summer of 2006 was a hot one, so Dad put the air conditioners in the windows right after Memorial Day.

Mandy was moping around the house. The muggy weather was really getting to her.

"I thought you cats loved the heat. You're always in the window sunbathing."

"I love the sun! What are you talking about?"

"Well, how come you're..."

"What? A little slower these days?"

"Well, yeah, I mean..."

"Henley, I'm no spring chicken."

"Stop talkin' like that."

"Listen, this morning when Dad took me to see Dr. Vaughn I got some medicine that proves I'm gettin' old."

"Medicine for what?"

"I have arthritis, some circulation problems..."

"Are you okay?"

"I just said... I have arth..."

"I heard you."

"Well then?"

"So, like... is this a bad thing?"

"Well, the news coulda been better, but I'll be all right."

"Are you sure?"

"Stop bein' such an old worry-wart!" She gave me the usual tail-swish in my face and then walked away up toward the staircase. I noticed she was walking a little slower and then I noticed that…

Oh, stop bein' such an old worry-wart! I said to myself.

Chapter Forty-Two

June was a beautiful month! The sun wasn't too hot, the humidity was lower, and the flowers in our window boxes looked like something straight out of The Royal Botanical Gardens.

The cats all loved sitting in the window when the flower boxes were in full bloom because birds and squirrels would come to the boxes and sit there. They weren't able to see the cats – but the cats saw them! They'd see blue jays, or robins, or starlings, and their tails would swish so hard you'd think they would fall right off.

I thought that was pretty funny.

One day Mom found her old Broadway CD from the musical CATS and she played it for us.

Mom bought it right after she saw the play at The Winter Garden Theatre in New York City about fifteen years ago. She patted me on the head. "It was a cool play, Hen… even if it *was* only about felines."

She always knows how to make me feel better.

Mom liked a song about Jellicle Cats. It was cute. I hope you get to hear it sometime.

Mandy liked the song 'Memory' best. When it played, she would sit right in front of the speaker and stay there until the last note had ended.

Memory...
All alone in the moonlight...
I can smile at the old days...
I was beautiful then...

Chapter Forty-Three

The 4th of July was soon upon us and Mom and Dad gave a great backyard bar-b-que for our friends and family. Mom came from a long line of great cooks, and Dad was no slouch himself! What a feast! Steaks, chicken, pork chops, hamburgers, hot dogs, grilled veggies, potato salad, macaroni salad, even tofu burgers for our Vegan friends. Like I said… a feast! Frankly, I was just interested in the steaks and hamburgers.

I had a great time! That is… until later in the evening when everyone drove over to Philadelphia to see the fireworks. Even though we live in another state, Center City, Philadelphia is just four miles away, right over the bridge, so I could hear every fiery boom that shot out over the sky. It reminded me of the thunder when I was a puppy, and I was kinda scared.

Mandy to the rescue.

"Think of happy things, Hen. The noise will only last for another ten minutes. You know that."

I shivered.

"Maybe it's only another eight minutes by now… maybe seven."

I stared at her.

"Think of it as a good memory."

"How?" I asked, with a shiver still in my spine.

"Don't think of the sadness attached to that sound, think of what it brought you."

"What are you saying?"

"I'm saying... it brought you Myra Glick... who brought you to Judy... who... "

I breathed a sigh of relief as she went on and on.

"Who brought you to Andrew... who then brought you to me, you lucky dog!"

I started to wag my butt.

"Hey, know what?"

"What?"

"There's a steak bone someone left that's just hanging out of that trash bag over there."

"There is?"

"Go look."

I walked over to the trash bag, and it was filled with empty paper cups and empty paper plates, and one still rather meaty steak bone. I grasped it ever so gingerly with my teeth and pulled it from the top of the bag.

"Know what?" Mandy stated.

"What?"

"You're pretty good at that."

"It's a dog thing."

"Know what else?"

"What?"

"The thundery noise stopped and you made your way through it just fine."

I stopped to listen.

No more thunder.

Amazing.

"I couldn't have done it without you, Miss Man-ners."

*"Sure you could! Now have at it. '**Bone**-appetit.'"*

She swished her tail at me and walked slowly back into the living room.

Chapter Forty-Four

July of 2006 was as hot a month as I could remember.

New Jersey is one sticky place in the summertime.

You know how they say, "It's not the heat, it's the humidity?"

...I think I get it now.

Mom was waiting for the repairman to fix the first floor air conditioning unit. Actually, I think I was in more of a hurry to see him than she was - 98 degrees with 97 percent humidity makes for a pretty sultry day.

Even Mookie, Ned, Miss Rose, and my Puppy Cat weren't their usual selves. The heat was getting to everybody.

I decided to go down to the basement where it was at least fifteen degrees cooler.

Apparently, Mandy had the same idea, and I noticed her the minute I walked down the steps.

"Hey, what's Little Mary Sunshine doing here?"

She stared at me, but didn't answer.

I looked around for one of the bones I usually leave in the basement, found it, and then sat down next to her.

"What's the matter?"

"I don't know."

"Yes, you do. Cats know all that stuff. Geez, even dogs know all that stuff! It's instinctual."

She looked me straight in the eyes. *"I'm dying, Hen."*

"YOU'RE WHAT?!"

"My legs get numb sometimes… it's getting harder to walk… I…"

"But you went to the vet! You got medicine!"

"I know, but I'm an old cat, Henley. You have to expect these things."

"How are you feeling now?"

"Truthfully?"

"Yeah."

"I feel sick. My legs are really cold."

"Are you in pain? I can bark and get Mom down here."

"I'm not really in pain, Hen. Don't bark for Mom, just let nature take its course."

I moved over closer to her and when my body brushed up against her back legs, I could feel how cold they were.

"What can I do for you?"

"You've always done right by me, Hen. There's nothing more for you to do."

Now I'm aware of the circle of life as much as any animal is. We have that gift. But somehow this was different. I was feeling the loss of her already and she was still with me. We sat in the basement for a while and reminisced about when we first met each other, when the kittens all came to live with us, our holidays, birthdays, and our wonderful parents. Then we talked about all the times that she would sit in the window when I was out in the car with Mom. Mandy would say she was just 'sunning herself,' when in truth, she was sitting there because she really missed me.

"I don't know what I can do, Mandy. I feel so helpless."

"Hen, it's all a part of the big plan. We come, we go. And hopefully in-between the comin' and goin' we've found some genuine love in our lives and some real friendships. That's what makes it easy to move on. A job well done... a life well spent."

I sighed. *"So, it's okay for you?"*

"Absolutely."

"And you've found that love and..."

"Of course, I have, Silly... I found you!"

I wagged my butt. *"And we'll see each other again someday?"*

"Do you canines know nothing?"

Again I sighed.

"Listen here, Sheepdog, we'll be together in that big happy piece of farmland in the sky someday. You'll see. Now go upstairs and leave me alone with my thoughts."

I moved from my spot next to her and started to walk up the basement steps.

"Hen?"

I turned and looked back at her, still sitting in the same position on the soft rug. *"What is it, Mandy?"*

"You're the best friend I ever had."

I dropped my head down, fearing that this might be the last thing she would ever say to me.

"And you're the best friend I ever had, Miss Man-ners."

... I turned and walked slowly up the steps.

Chapter Forty-Five

Mom wrapped Mandy in a warm blanket and cuddled her in her arms as she called my Dad.

Again, I heard one half of the conversation, but I knew 100% of what was going on.

"Andrew! I went downstairs to do some laundry and Mandy was just sitting there on the floor. I called her and she didn't come to me. ... No. ... Her legs are like ice. ... She can't even stand on them! ... I did, I called Dr. Vaughn right before I called you! ... I know, I know. ... I have her in my arms. ... No, no pain. She's not crying. ... Okay. Okay. See you in ten minutes."

Mom turned toward Mandy and cuddled her closer in her arms. "Dad's on his way, Sweetheart. We'll take you to Dr. Vaughn. We'll do everything we can..."

Mom started to cry. I snuggled myself into her knees. She patted me on the head with her free hand.

Poor Mom.

I don't know when they all appeared, but the next thing I knew, Mookie, Ned, Miss Rose, and Cynthia were all in the dining room with us.

Mom sat in the chair nearest the living room and held Mandy close, rocking her ever so gently. "You'll be all right, Sweetheart. You'll be all right. Daddy's on his way."

Cynthia looked confused. *"What's happening?"*

Rose sniffed at Mandy's soft, pink blanket.

Ned circled the chair.

Mookie sat on the stairs and watched Mandy like a hawk.

"Isn't anyone gonna answer me?!"

"She's going to die," Mookie announced.

Cynthia looked up at Mandy. *"Are you?! Are you going to die?!"*

"It's my time, Cyn. And it's okay. Dying isn't the end, it's part of a new beginning."

Mandy did her best to comfort Cynthia who was quite distraught.

"We have nine lives. Remember them saying that? Well, I have to move on. I have eight more comin' to me."

Bless her heart, I thought. *She always finds a way to soothe others, no matter how bad she's feeling herself. Whatta cat!*

Ned rubbed up against the chair and Rose sniffed the blanket once again.

"Now go along. Go upstairs and find a nice sunny window and think good thoughts of me."

Rose, Ned, and Cynthia did as they were told by the Queen of the House.

Mookie hung out on the steps.

Mandy looked up at him. *"You're a pretty smart little fellow,"* she said.

117

"Farm instincts."

"Well, you keep using those instincts and you'll always land on your feet."

"I'm a cat. I'm always gonna land on my feet!"

Mookie ran down the steps and nuzzled Mandy's face and then ran back up the steps to join his friends.

Just then Dad walked in the door. He had the saddest look on his face. I was always used to him being so cheerful and smiley.

Poor Dad.

The minute Mandy saw him she let out the only 'meow' I had heard from her in days. Mom was still visibly upset when Dad took Mandy from her arms. He felt her legs. They were as cold as ice. "Oh, Mandy girl," he sighed as his eyes started to fill.

"We'd better go. Dr. Vaughn's waiting for us." Mom sniffled.

Dad turned toward me. "Be a good boy, Hen."

I usually made eye contact when my Dad talked to me, but I couldn't stop looking at Mandy.

"You heard what he said," Miss Man-ners stated. *"Be a good boy, Hen."*

"I will."

I watched Dad wrap her up in her soft pink blanket in a more comfortable position and then the three of them headed for the door.

Mandy turned one last time to look at me.

"I love you, Henley. See you on the other side."

"I love you, too, Mandy. See you on the other side."

The door closed, I heard Mom turn the key in the lock, and then they walked up the driveway. The car was parked on the side of the house, and I glued myself to the open window. The light streaming in was very bright and hard on my eyes, but I sat there looking out of it just the same.

Then, I heard her voice once again.

"Sunning yourself?... Or are you just gonna miss me?"

Chapter Forty-Six

Two hours later I heard our car pull up into the driveway.

I walked to the open window on the side of the house.

The car drew to a stop.

I saw Mom get out.

Then I saw Dad get out.

But I didn't see Mandy.

I watched as my Dad walked toward the back of the car. He opened the door and then he took out a medium-sized white box. He handled it ever so gently. I watched him as he carried the box slowly toward the back of the house.

I heard him cry.

I noticed a soft pink blanket sticking out over one of the corners.

Mandy...

Chapter Forty-Seven

I can hardly recall the first week after Mandy died. By week number two, I was a bit more of my old self and the fog had lifted, slightly – the kitties were about the same.

By the third week, we were all back into the swing of things physically, but in our hearts, we were all just going through the motions.

How many times have you heard, "It's JUST a dog," or, "It's JUST a cat!"

Well, for some people it is. But to people like our mom and dad, we were all family. Not "just a dog" or "just a cat"... we were family. And that's the way I felt about all of the cats, too – they were my family. They sure were.

On the one month anniversary of Mandy's death, Mom and Dad placed a small memorial stone on her grave in the backyard. Rose, Cynthia, Mookie, and Ned watched from the dining room window, but I got to go outside and see what was going on.

The stone was placed in the prettiest part of the garden, right under a beautiful sixty-foot pine tree that was surrounded by ivy, winding morning glory, and tall amethyst-colored iris.

Dad patted my head. "She was a great cat, Henley."

I wagged my butt. *She sure was.*

Mom planted a few geraniums around the stone and when the planting was over we all took a step back to have a look.

I saw Dad wipe his eyes.

So did Mom.

I walked close to the grave once again and then Dad said to me, "Know what the stone says, Hen?"

And then he read to me the words that were etched upon that stone, the words that would be forever etched upon my soul:

A true friend

leaves footprints

in your heart.

Chapter Forty-Eight

Although Miss Rose, Ned, Mookie, and my Puppy Cat, Cynthia, had a good grip on each of their lives - all nine of them - there was still a leadership position that was empty since Mandy passed away. I figured Mookie would step up to the plate, but, well, cats always do their own thing, and I guess it just wasn't the right time, so they chose me until their own pecking order had been decided.

"What do we do now, Hen?" Cynthia asked.

"We go about our lives, it's..."

"The circle of life," Mookie finished.

"That's right, Mook," I said. *"And, we make the best of every day we have left."*

Ned was usually the quiet kitty, but when he spoke, he spoke from his heart. *"And we should never forget to be thankful for the kind people who took us in and loved us."*

I then added, *"Yes. And let's hope and pray that lots of other people learn to do the same thing for all the other animals left out there."*

Cynthia's voice was soft and gentle. *"Yeah, the ones like we used to be."*

Rose finished her sister's thought. *"Lonely, scared, abused, hungry..."*

"Yup," I agreed. *"A little love would go a long way."*

"Ya know, sometimes," Mookie said, *"it's hard for people to make room for needy pets, humans live such hectic lives and..."*

"Yeah, that's true, but, well... maybe I could..." I hesitated.

"What, Hen? Could what?"

I turned my head to the left and then to the right. *"Well, maybe I'll write a book about all this stuff someday, and then..."*

"A BOOK?!! You're a crazy old dog." Mookie swished his tail at me.

Cynthia snuggled her face into my paw. *"Yeah, you are, Hen... but we love you anyway!"*

I then watched as my four friends scampered up the steps to cozy beds, fuzzy toys, and deliciously soft down pillows.

As for me?

I sat down by the beautiful open window on the side of the house, just taking in the day...

... sunning myself.

Mookie

Rose

Ned

Cynthia
(My Puppy Cat)

and

Mandy

Acknowledgments

I would like to thank Mom for typing this for me, and Dad for making a few necessary changes, but most of all, I want to thank them for loving me.

I would also like to thank all of the wonderful people and their animal friends that I've known in my lifetime:

Jon-Boy, Krissy, Crispin Crispian, Mont, "Myra", Leon and Nan West and Patches and Pippa, Bill "Hayner or No" West, Laura, Doug, Molly, Ian, Myles and the late great Murphy Van Wieren, Lou, Francisco, and their sweet Daisy, Aunt Viva and her doggies, Rico and Rosa, Adam Junker and his cat, Sophie, Richard Floyd, to Franny, Shelly, Dudley, and Corey Rose, their cat, Rocky & Rocky's dog, Elwood, Editor extraordinaire, Alex Hill and his cat, Dusty, thanks also to Ruth, Donna, Mallory, Harris, Nee-uss, Blondie, Teddy, to my pal Stan, to Bobby Wags (who always calls me Helmsley or Barkley), and for "Schnapps", to Betsy and her Sadie girl, Jimi Pru and his darling dogs, Boo & Tia, Freddy and Gabriella & The Poppets: Peanut and Jean Luc, also to Grannie Annie and Charlie, to Donna, Victor, and

Baby Girl, for Boomie, Pouncie Boo-Boo, and Leo, to Genevieve, Lauren, Gregory & "Sassy", for Mary, and her Milo, to Maryann, Theresa, Andrew, Quenton, and Harley, and to Raymond and Carol Burke and their dog, the late great Rusty Burke, also to Brigitte and Heike's dear cats: Finn and Pauli, Adrienne & Dusty, to Hope Doms and her cat Fonzie, for Ruthie's Lois and her sweetheart pooch, Kato, for Mr. and Mrs. Utley and Etana, as well as for Norm Washington and his Daisy and, to Buttons, Chris, Suzie, Cyn, and Ralph. And... to all of the other great dogs, cats, bunnies, sheep, and horses who became my friends over the years. And, also to my Mom's much loved sheepdogs of the past who helped her to understand dogs like me: Martha, Charlie, Fred, Winston, Harry, and Addison. And to Cromwell, who graced the town of Merchantville, New Jersey with his glorious sheepdog presence for over sixteen years, and, to his loving and devoted parents, Bill and Tam DeGregory.

Most of all I would like to thank: Miss Rose, Mookie, Ned, my Puppy Cat, Cynthia, and of course, Mandy, for allowing me to be a part of such a kind, caring, and devoted pack.

Written with much love, loyalty, and affection -

Henley Harrison West
May 31st, 2007

Part of the proceeds from the royalties of this book will be donated to:

Almost Home Animal Shelter
9140C Pennsauken Highway
Pennsauken, NJ 08109
Phone: (856) 663-3058
E-mail: almosthomeshelter@comcast.net

NEOESR, Inc.
New England Old English Sheepdog Rescue, Inc.
49 Stonehedge
Lincoln, Massachusetts 01773
Home Page: http://www.neoesr.org
Hotline: 781-259-8173
Fax: 781-259-0720

and
The SPCA of Philadelphia
(where Mom's family adopted their first dog back in 1957!)
350 East Erie Avenue
Philadelphia, Pennsylvania. 19134
215.426.6300
www.pspca.org

My Friends...

The ASPCA! The ASPCA was founded in 1866 as the first humane organization in the Western Hemisphere. The Society was formed to alleviate the injustices animals faced then, and they continue to battle cruelty today. Whether it's saving a pet who has been accidentally poisoned, fighting to pass humane laws, rescuing animals from abuse or sharing resources with shelters across the country, the ASPCA works toward the day in which no animal will live in pain or fear. Please join them in the fight to end animal cruelty—become an ASPCA Member today!

www.aspca.org

ASPCA
24-Hour Animal Poison Information!!!
If your pet has swallowed anything you fear is poisonous, please call the ASPCA's National Poison Control Center:
888-426-4435
This is a toll-free call!

The SPCA of Philadelphia
350 East Erie Avenue
Philadelphia, Pennsylvania. 19134
215.426.6300
www.pspca.org

The PSPCA addresses the needs of thousands of homeless animals a year. They started out with a single center in Philadelphia and, with the help of dedicated staff and generous donors, burgeoned into a state-wide operation with seven very busy shelters.

Please become a supporter and help this marvelous organization continue to materialize their mission, helping not only animals in need but also inspiring people to be more humane. Bring out the best in yourself. Adopt a pet!

Petfinder.com

The Petfinder.com Foundation helps support the thousands of animal organization members of Petfinder.com by raising funds for them. Their object? To increase the number of homeless pets adopted.

Petfinder changes lives. They affect not only the four-footed animals waiting to be adopted, but also the people who care for them. They supply equipment and funds so that thousands of homeless pets have healthier and happier lives and thousands of shelter and rescue folks can do their jobs better. Please make a donation today and visit their wonderful website often.

Pets911(pets to adopt in your area!!!)
Pets911.com

Shelter and rescue organizations in this country are brimming with unwanted, stray and homeless pets. Please do your part to help alleviate this problem. With everyone understanding the issue, doing their part to care for their pets like family members, and utilizing the important resources PETS 911 can offer your community, we can and will solve this issue!

If you don't have Internet access, adoption and care information is available via the PETS 911 toll-free, bi-lingual phone line at 1-888-PETS-911

Net Pets...

An index of cat humane societies and **shelters** listed by state and cat breed **rescue** groups listed by location and breed. There's a kitty out there just waiting for you!

www.netpets.com/cats/catresc.html

Best Friends...
www.bestfriends.org

Best Friends works with you and with humane groups all across the country to bring about a time when homeless, unwanted animals are no longer being destroyed in shelters, and when every healthy dog or cat can be guaranteed a good life in a caring home. Please contact them today!

WAGS Rescue and Referral

The purpose of **WAGS** is to match people with dogs and puppies who lost their homes or never had one, through no fault of their own, including: natural disasters, poverty, negligence, abuse, and relocation.

Contact: Kim & Stephen Leslie - 267.205.8344/8244
Angela & Adam Malerman   - 267.626.3885
Sandy, Tony, & Anthony Lang - 215.357.2963
wagsrescue@aol.com
Web site: www.wagsrescue.com

AND… In case you're thinking about adopting a sheepdog like me… please note: Old English Sheepdogs are high maintenance dogs. Our large body size combined with volumes of hair often causes many sheepdogs to end up in "Rescue." In other words, we're really cute… but it takes a **lot** of work to care for us in the right way.

There are rescue shelters for *every* dog breed. Check your local phone directory, or search online if you would like to rescue a specific breed.

Please remember:

Always report animal abuse of any kind. You **must** be the voice for these dear, sweet animals who cannot speak for themselves.

Also… please have all of your companion pets spayed or neutered and *always* make sure your pet is up to date with his or her shots!

We want to stay healthy so we can be around to love you for a long, long, long, long time!

Your Shaggy Friend...

 Henley

He is your friend, your partner, your defender, your dog.

You are his life, his love, his leader.

He will be yours, faithful and true, to the last beat of his heart.

You owe it to him to be worthy of such devotion.

LaVergne, TN USA
16 November 2009
164190LV00003B/11/A